MW01504097

Sweet Surrender

Sweet Surrender

Series One

ATINUKE DUROJAIYE

XULON PRESS

Xulon Press Elite
2301 Lucien Way #415
Maitland, FL 32751
407.339.4217
www.xulonpress.com

Unless otherwise indicated, Scripture quotations taken from the King James Version (KJV)–*public domain*.

Paperback ISBN-13: 978-1-66288-032-2
Dust Jacket ISBN-13: 978-1-66288-033-9
Ebook ISBN-13: 978-1-66288-034-6

DEDICATION

To God be all the glory. This is the Lord's doing; it is marvelous in our eyes. Psalm 118:23 (KJV)

Thank God, for family, fellowship, friendship, food, and the dinner table.

To God be all the glory.

This is the Lord's doing and it is marvelous in our eyes. (Psalm 118:23 NCB emphasis added)

Thank God for family, fellowship, friendship, and food.

CONTENTS

ONE

Mabel has been so excited since the moment she received the call from the multinational company where she'd applied to, to resume the position of a secretary on Monday with immediate effect. The news made her nervous and happy at the same time. After graduating from the Department of Mass Communication in the well-known University of Port Harcourt, located in the Choba district of Port Harcourt, in Rivers State, Nigeria, about a year ago. This news of her appointment was a big flex and a huge celebration for her family. Her parents had managed through hardship and debt just to see her go through school, with the hope of having a brighter future. With this job Mabel drew closer to her bright future than she'd ever been.

When she'd received the text at her home in Kuruama, a small town located on the Bonny Island, she ran all the way to the river side, her feet felt lighter, as if her eyes, now that she was using them, gave her extra lightness. She ran past the Masters' bungalow that held homes for the primary school teachers and corp members serving in the village.

She passed the side garden adjacent to the Anglican church her family attended and, eager to share the good news, she shot into the tarred road which led to the beach, where her father laid his fishing nets.

"Papa! Papa!" she screamed when she caught the sight of him from a distance. She could see the excitement sparkling in Pa. Ebiye's eyes the moment she broke the good news to him.

"Eh Nana owei nua," he had said as he danced at the river bank. His feet dug deep into the wet sand forming several duplicate shapes of his massive feet, as he proceeded with each step. As Mabel watched him in amazement, a smile swept across her face. She quickly helped Pa. Sekibo packed his fishing nets and cutlass and they made their way home.

During this time Mabel was at school, her family survived on the proceeds of Papa's fishing and the little farm products her mother brought home. On this day she led her father by the hand like a little child who is just about taking his first steps. His fishing backpack, made from sack and a little rod pierced through both sides, dangled in her left hand as she walked, swinging it in different directions. This was all the happiness they needed, a breakthrough for all of them.

"God indeed answers prayers," her mother had said when she returned from the farm.

"Yes, Mama," Mabel responded, clasping her hands together.

"So, when do you leave for Port Harcourt?" Papa asked curiously.

"First thing tomorrow morning." Mabel responded

There was deep relief on Mama's face as she lit the fire with a burning broom bristle. Papa laid on his armchair outside waiting for mama to finish with the dinner preparation. The night was inaccessibly dark. For the past weeks the moon has been rising later and later every night until it was only seen at dawn.

Whenever this happened the nights were as black as charcoal while the early mornings had the brightness of a full-blown day. Mabel and her mother sat on a mat on the floor in their kitchen hut, after having their dinner of Onunu and Catfish soup. A palm oil lamp gave out yellowish light that spread only to a certain angle of the hut, making it a bit difficult for them to see who might be standing at the entrance of the hut. There was an oil lamp in their main building which stood in front of the kitchen hut. The reflection made the building look like a soft yellow half-eye set in the solid massiveness of the night.

By now the world was quiet, except for the ear-piercing cry of insects, which was absolutely a part of the night, and the sounds from the neighbor who lived a few meters from Pa. Sekibo's compound pounding flour with huge mortar and pestle. Everyone knew the sound of Mama Tari's mortar and pestle. She would go out during the day to gossip at another neighbor's house, then come back at night to make food for her family.

The sound of her huge mortar and pestle were also part of the night.

"Mabel . . ." her father called. He has a way of adding an invisible /I/ sound at the beginning of her name. It was his mother tongue. Mabel rose quickly from the mat where she sat beside her mother. She made to dust off the invisible sand from her dress as she came out of the kitchen hut to meet her father.

"Yes. Papa," she responded when she was already standing in front of him. He beckoned her to take her seat on the little log bench he'd made from the coconut tree gotten from the beach some months ago. He cleared his throat before saying any more words: "Now you have gotten a job with a big company, which is very good news to all of us, but where are you going to stay in Port Harcourt? Because we all know that you can not travel through the ocean to the city every day." He made this statement without any emotions on his face.

Mabel smiled, exposing her gap tooth, "I have a friend in Port Harcourt and all arrangements have been made for me to live with her till I'm able to get my own place."

"Oh! It's okay then." "Besides, you know the city more than we do." He said chuckling, "May God go with you and you must never forget where you come from,"

"I know, Papa, and I will not bring back trouble." Mabel laughed as she stood up to leave, taking Papa's emptied plates along with her own to the kitchen. She only needed to pack a few things in a bag before going to bed since she doesn't really have much to wear. She can get a few more clothes in the city.

Mabel has not been able to bring herself to sleep. She had spent the early part of the night after eating praying and thanking God for the good news. It was past 3:00 a.m. from the time on her watch, yet she felt so uneasy and nervous about her journey in the morning. Traveling on the Bonny waters can be hectic and dangerous, and sometimes stories of sea pirates and kidnappings are heard, but that wasn't her portion. Mabel knew that if she didn't sleep now it will be difficult for her to stay awake during her six hours journey to the city on the Bonny ocean.

One time she had tried sleeping and she had found herself drowning deep in the ocean. She jerked out of sleep clutching her Bible to her chest as she mouthed the words "The blood of Jesus" to herself.

Mabel had stretched herself and scratched the spot on her thigh where a mosquito had bitten her as she slept. Another one was lurking around her left arm buzzing and wailing. She slapped the arm and hoped she had killed it.

Mabel turned on her side and went back to sleep. She was aroused in the morning by her mother who always woke to each new day without any alarm set by her side. Mabel quickly got ready and set out to meet the first boat to the city. Her parents bade her goodbye as the boat began to sail far into the ocean.

She arrived in the city of Port Harcourt at around three minutes past four o'clock in the evening. At the park she bought a big loaf of bread for her friend Chika, which is a customary gift for travelers to bring their loved ones. When she arrived at the apartment at Trans-woji, she could smell the city life once again.

"You're welcome, my good friend," Chika told her for the one hundred and ninety-ninth time.

"Thank you, my sister. If not that you had agreed to let me stay here, I don't know what I would've done."

"You helped me too during school days, so this shouldn't be a big deal, besides what are friends for?"

"Abi o, my sister." They both laughed. Both ladies enjoyed the rest of the evening gisting and chatting about life in general.

The fizzling sound from her rickety phone made Mabel jump out of bed. After a short prayer she hurriedly went into the bathroom for a quick bath. She quickly dressed herself in a grey skirt and a white collar top. Her dark kinky hair neatly brushed and tied into a bun at the top center of her head. She hastily walked out of her street to the nearest park to board a taxi to her office, which was almost thirty minutes away.

The yellow morning sun burned through the light fog hovering above the city, exposing giant oaks along the roadside, well-trimmed lawns, and a large array of granite and glass structures.

The city of more than five million inhabitants was already awake and buzzing in the early hours of the morning. Traffic jams were already beginning to form and school children were trotting happily, chit-chatting on their way to school. It was all calm, yet so busy. Mabel checked her phone for the time, it read 8:30 a.m., and the resumption time for her position was at 9:00 a.m.

"Oh God," she exclaimed. The cab moved some distance without any traffic jam until she was just a few meters away from the office headquarters.

"Take" she said, handing the cash over to the driver as she alights from the car. The driver grabbed the money from her and pointed to the direction of the company building. "You fit Waka go there" he said in Nigerian Pidgin English.

"Okay, thank you," Mabel responded as she ran as fast as she could. Within two minutes she was in the building. She waved past the security guard and headed straight for the main door. She pulled the glass door aggressively only to find herself colliding into a man, right in front of her. He was tall, about 6' 2", handsome, and very muscular in his blue suit and trousers.

"Watch where you're going," he barked at her, his voice booming in the empty entrance hall.

"I'm sorry," Mabel offered.

"You should be sorry for yourself," he said, pushing her to the left then adjusting his suit before moving forward. He banged the door after he'd passed. She watched him go out through the door into his car then she suddenly remembered she had just two minutes left to clock in. Mabel walked straight down the empty hall to the reception.

"You must be Mabel?

"Yes, Mabel Sekibo," she replied, wiping off the beads of sweat that had now formed on her face with a white handkerchief.

"Okay, that's the way to your office, your supervisor is already there, She will show you to your desk."

"Thank you, Ma'am," she said and walked through the lobby to the office on the right.

TWO

Heading a company is not as easy as it seems. For Kabiri Dan-Dagogo, it's been a really tough journey since he inherited the company from his father three years ago. His father, Mr. Temple Dagogo, had left a legacy for his first son, which he was expected to emulate. Sometimes, Kabiri had wondered how his father was able to manage all three businesses.

The hotels and restaurants didn't give him as much problems as TEMS Oil and Gas. Kabiri Dan-Dagogo is strong, brave, and fearless, but he doesn't have as much capacity to handle some matters effectively as his father had. There has not been much change from what his father had left for him. And, as the sole heir to the inheritance, he has to be consistent and put in all the work to continue the long tradition of the family name. He is an only son and a pampered brat. His mother had told him to be as smart as a tortoise and as strong as a lion. He is the CEO now and the burden and pressure would rest on his shoulders. Although he acts fierce and mean to his staff, he shows a tiny part of his good self to Amina, his girlfriend.

Amina is also from a wealthy family, the daughter of the minister of finance in Nigeria. When Kabiri had met her in California, he had fallen deeply for her. Despite his ego, and pride, he has always put Amina as top priority. He would send her huge amounts of money for trips and vacations. Just on her recent birthday, he got her a BMW-M5, worth millions of Naira.

Nothing was a secret in TEMS Oil and Gas. The boss was always uptight with his staff, yet his private affairs seem to be at the fingertips of his workers, including the gateman. It's rumored that he's spent enormous sums of money on trips and vacations and has a dozen expensive cars he barely even uses. His few friends and associates have always known him to be a reckless spender. Alex, his closest friend, never gets tired of warning him about his spending habits, but Kabiri always had a way of waving away the advice.

"It's my money. I work for it and I can spend it the way I please. Relax, man, there's more where all these are coming from," he would always say.

Three weeks after resuming her position at TEMS, Mabel and her colleagues were called to the conference room by their boss. The newly employed staff had all resumed during the week he'd been traveling, and it was only appropriate that he'd try to get to see those working in the secretarial team and the other departments. The meeting was scheduled for 10:00 o'clock. The senior staff were already seated around the table, except for one empty seat, which stood at the head of the conference table. Clearly, that empty seat belonged to the CEO without being told.

Mabel was busy scrolling through her phone as others formed little discussion groups. The door creaked open softly and everyone stood up except Mabel, who was so engrossed in the news she was reading from her cell phone.

"Mabel, stand up," the voice said to her, almost in a whisper, accompanied by a tap on her shoulder.

"Oops!" Mabel jumped out of her seat; all eyes were on her. The boss had walked to his seat at this point without her notice and had his gaze fixed on her. As she locked eyes with him, his stare sent shivers down her spine. There was her boss, the owner of the company, right in front of her. The shock didn't let her speak; she stared at him slowly lowering her gaze from his face down to the table, but he didn't flinch, not even for a second.

"You may all sit please," he said.

He adjusted his tie a bit and continued speaking. He had an expressionless face that was so serious that an observer could barely know what was on his mind. The door opened a little and a young elegant lady walked in.

She was dressed in really sophisticated clothes. Her bag was the latest Chanel edition, topped with twenty-two inches of bone straight hair. She had a perfect blend of green and yellow acrylic nails sitting gorgeously on her finger nails. They were long and Mabel wondered if she could truly cook with those sharp-pointed nails. As far as Mabel was concerned, ladies who wore extremely long nails were lazy in the kitchen. She was a black goddess of beauty; she was class and definitely a perfect march for Kabiri.

"Hey, Love, you didn't tell me you were coming?" He said, as he went over and pressed a warm kiss on both of her cheeks.

"I called you, but you weren't picking up. I decided to stop by, since I'm already in the neighborhood," she responded in a chilling, soft voice, tender enough to make a man trip over.

"Oh!"

"I'm so sorry, Love," he replied. Both were ignoring the people sitting in the room. It was their moment.

"Uhm! I'm having a meeting with my staff; I will see you in the evening Okay?"

"Fine then." She said, dangling her keys so everyone could hear the sound of the keys clicking on themselves.

After they had finished with their little PDA session, she closed the door behind her as she left, while Kabiri returned to his seat. He examined their faces a little before proceeding with the meeting.

Every man had a soft spot, and this lady seemed to have the keys to his sweet side.

The meeting continued.

THREE

T he meeting didn't last as long as Mabel had anticipated. The presence of her new boss makes her rather uncomfortable and she hoped she would not have to share any space with him ever again. This was the same man who almost pushed her to the ground the first day she resumed. She tried to flash back if she ever added "Sir" to the words she said to him the first day she'd met him. She could feel the goosebumps creeping into her skin again. Her heart pounded so loudly that when it got to her turn to introduce herself, Mabel stuttered and couldn't make simple coherent sentences. She was given a new MacBook Pro 2020 Intel i7 for her official use, and so were the other new staff members. She had it packed into her bag and made to exit the conference room when she was asked to meet the boss in his office.

She paused, her heart almost popping out of her chest. "Come with a copy of your CV." He had told her. His husky voice filled the entire room. The moment she heard her name she knew she was in trouble, big trouble, and it seemed too early for her boss to notice any unwelcome attitude. She wasn't optimistic about the call and knew that whatever it was that warranted the summons, it wasn't good. She could feel deep down in her spirit that all wasn't well. From the look of things, Mr. Kabiri wasn't a friend to any of his staff, as they all trembled whenever he spoke just like she did. She stopped by her office and put down the bag she'd been holding. She wasn't ready to swallow all that awkward moment along with a heavy bag in her hand.

She knocked on his office door twice before turning the knob and to her greatest surprise, the other two selected staff were already seated. She gently closed the door to avoid the loud creaky sound as she examined the room with her eyes. It was a really nice space with such cool ambience for a grumpy man like her boss. His office was a really cool, chic, and expensive space, twice the size of the one she shared with her colleagues, Kate, the main secretary, and Timi.

Kabiri's office has very fancy expensive leather seats and a huge, mahogany office desk, wall-to-wall carpeting, completely blue, with shades of grey outlines, a creamy-dreamy, a beautiful seating area for guests with an oval glass coffee table, making the office really alluring and intimidating, giving it a very rich aura, with expensive paintings hanging on the pale cream walls. The windows were huge and wide, allowing sunshine from outside to light up the room with natural light, adding elegance to the room beautifully. The whole room is translucent and warm. The office also has a three-door filing cabinet on one wall and a good number of compartments below it, where he puts some of the files and other official stuff.

"Why are you always late?" He finally said, breaking the silence that lingered in the room as Mabel walked in.

"Sir?" She said, pretending not to hear him the first time. She joined the others who were seated in front of the boss. They all handed him their CV one after the other, then he surveyed them and asked a few questions to those concerned. Mabel was seated there wondering why he hadn't said anything about hers until he asked the others to excuse them.

"I asked a question earlier and you didn't respond, Mabel." He said more like a query in his tone.

"Um," she stuttered.

"Why are you always late?"

"I'm sorry, Sir," she replied with her eyes down on her thighs. She twisted her fingers around each other preventing them from shaking vehemently. This seemed like a very long period of torture, but for what she knows nothing about.

"Mabel Sekibo, that's your name?" He asked, searching her face for a response as he tossed and flipped the two-page CV vigorously, as though he wanted to see something else.

"Yes Sir, Mabel Sekibo," she answered with her eyes locked to him. She didn't intend looking so deeply into his eyes, but somehow she couldn't get her eyes off his face. He had the most daring look she'd ever seen, and it made her really uncomfortable. The heat from his stare seemed capable of melting her skin like cubes of sugar placed on a heater.

"Who employed you here?" he asked.

"Sir?"

"I . . . I, em," she kept stuttering trying to figure out the best real answer for this question but she couldn't find the words. She had just been kicked off guard. He knew what he was doing. This was his deliberate attempt to humiliate her.

"Your CV says you are a graduate of Mass Communication" he said in a tone that seems to be more of a statement than an actual question.

"Yes Sir," she answered, still staring blankly at her boss.

"I see . . ." he cleared his throat repeatedly.

"Where are you from?"

"Kalabari . . ."

"I can see that from your name. What part of Kalabari are you from? That is what I want to know?"

"Kuruama, in Bonny local government area." She said plainly. He studied her face for a short time, pausing as though he was certainly thinking of the next thing to say, an awful thing in a soothing manner. He cleared his throat like he had swallowed a lump the night before.

"You see, Mabel, this is a big multinational organization, and we try as much as we can to employ experienced and competent people to manage the affairs of each department as a team, but your CV says you have no prior experience whatsoever. You are not supposed to be in this organization in the first place.

"I inherited this business from my father, and if I keep employing amateurs like you, in less than three years the company would be in a shit hole. Do you understand my point?"

Of course she didn't, but she had to nod anyway. She didn't have the slightest idea what her employment had to do with the sermon he's given her now. The company called her and told her she had been offered employment, so what is all this?

"Please, Sir," Mabel said, her knees on the ground, "I am just a poor girl who's trying to survive out here. I have aging parents who solely depend on me for food. I will put in my very best sir, I don't even want a raise…" she continued stuttering all the way through, "this pay is enough for me and I am willing to learn all about the job, Sir, please I beg you." Tears rolled down her eyes as she appealed to her boss with her palms placed together as though she's in a serious prayer session with both knees still kissing the ground.

He kept quiet for a while without a single expression on his face, then he asked her to stand up.

He handed the CV back to her. "You'll be working under close supervision for some time, but the moment I realize you are not improving, you're leaving this company for good. Is that clear?" He asked rhetorically. She nodded, even though she did fully understand the reason for this. She stood up and left the office. During lunch break, she spent her time in the bathroom praying and studying the Word. She had no one else but God Himself, who had made all men in His own image.

Lord, you said in Your Word in Proverbs 21 verse 1 that the hearts of kings are in your hands. I do not know what's going on, but I believe that

Your thoughts for me are thoughts of good and not of evil to give me an expected end. according to Jeremiah 29:11. Take control, Lord. Amen.

She placed both hands on the toilet sink, then turned on the tap and splashed water on her face. She wanted a job, that was all she wanted, this wasn't what she'd expected to face each day; a toxic place, with a toxic boss, was way out of the line. What was she going to tell her parents if she lost the only thing that has brought smiles to their faces in the last couple of months? There had to be a way out but what way exactly. She couldn't figure it out. What exactly could be the problem? Mabel thought to herself. She'd only been employed a few weeks ago, and she hadn't experienced any trouble with work, or her head of department, not until this boss showed up. From the very day she'd met him in that meeting, she knew he had something against her, something only he knew. She dried her hands with a small napkin and went back to the office.

She was the only new employee in her department and was assigned to report to the main head of the department. They all had reports to make at the end of the week and each person must submit their reports directly to the main boss. As she pulled out her seat, Mabel noticed her supervisor watching her. The look on her face wasn't a friendly one, but that's the least of the troubles on Mabel's mind. She could deal with a nasty supervisor, but definitely not a grumpy department head.

FOUR

The sun poured through Mabel's window. One more day had unfolded, bringing with it new expectations and goals. The gleam of the first light saturated her room. Mabel scoured her blurred eyes and strolled to the window. There was a silvery sparkle overhead. The main beams of daylight illuminated the room in its vastness. The sunrise tune of melodic birdsong floated in as the rising sun cast a ruddy tint across the morning sky. Brilliant fingers of daylight adorned the scene. The blue sky was speckled with fleecy white mists that floated languidly on the delicate breeze. The periodic yelping of cars and reeving engines could be heard from meters away. Dappled sun radiated through the trees, making baffling shadows, as the first barking dogs ended the quietness of the new day. Mabel stretched the laziness out of her body. Still in her pajamas, she picked up her Bible from the side table where she had left it the night before.

"Oh, thank You, Jesus," she yawned deeply, stretching herself some more. She flipped through the Bible and finally got the chapter and verse she was looking for, Isaiah 41:10. She traced her finger through every word and meditated on it for a few more minutes. This is Your Word, Lord, and I need Your help now. Take total control of my work, take control of my boss's mind. Guide my thoughts that I will always please You with my deeds. Amen.

Just when she had concluded her prayers, Chika came knocking at her door, when there was no response she pushed the door open slightly and walked in.

"Oh! You're awake already?"

"Yes, I am."

"Good morning" Mabel greeted Chika and stood up from the bed where she'd been sitting.

"We have laundry to do this morning, remember?" Chika reminded.

"Of course, I didn't forget, I will be out soon so we can start."

"Okay then," Chika replied and strode out of the room. Mabel then selected the clothes she needed to wash and put them in the laundry basket. She also changed the bed cover as it was due for the week. She took the clothes to the laundry room and carefully placed each item into the washer. She added some washing powder and turned on the machine.

"Have you ever had a mean boss?" Mabel asked. Chika gave her a confused look, rolling her eyes from one end to the other like tiny balls.

"Arrh! A mean boss?" She repeated after Mabel, who gave her a still nod in reply.

"Well, to be honest, I haven't tasted one." They both laughed at the statement.

"C'mon talk to me. What's the problem? Are you having a hard time at work?"

"Yes." Mabel answered without letting the question drop. "I think my job is threatened as we speak."

"Threatened! By whom?"

"The boss." Mabel responded coldly.

"Don't mind them. That's exactly how they treat new employees just because they've worked for longer years and are now used to the system. Don't worry, you will soon fit in."

"No, Chika, you're getting it all wrong. My boss, the CEO of TEMS Oil and Gas, is the one with all the troubles. Since he returned after his trip, it's been one complaint or another. Did you know, the other day he told me he would fire me the next time he finds out I'm not doing my job effectively?" Mabel let out a heavy sigh, "I'm confused and honestly I don't know what to do"

"Hey, girl, you don't have to be like that. Listen, he might not see what you're doing now, but trust me, sooner or later he will be happy he let you work in his company. You are smart, and you shouldn't let anyone make you feel less of yourself." Mabel nodded as Chika reached out to her, "Come here."

Chika welcomed Mabel into her arms and gave her a reassuring hug. "C'mon, wipe that look off your face. He's just . . ."

"My phone . . ." Mabel cut in, interrupting what her friend was about to say. She ran quickly into the other room.

Mr. Dagogo? Why was he calling at this time of the day? It's too early to ruin my day. She had a debate in her mind whether or not to take this call. She walked with the phone ringing in her hand back to where she had been standing with her friend. Then she finally decided to answer, after the fifth ring. She switched the call on speaker, so Chika would also hear what her boss had to say.

"Hello, Sir."

"Mabel, how are you?" The husky voice spoke from the other end of the phone.

"I'm fine. Good morning, Sir."

"A quick one, I will be having a meeting at 7:00 p.m. today, Hotel Presidential conference hall, Aba Road, GRA Phase II, and so I want you to accompany me to that meeting. Dress nice."

"Okay, Sir but . . ." she said, scratching her head.

"But what? The other secretaries? Well, I don't want them. There are no buts, okay." When Dagogo gives you an instruction you obey without complaints and buts. "Do you understand?"

"Yes, Sir . . ." she answered in a rather shaky voice as he ended the call.

"You see? What I told you just a few minutes ago, he doesn't care about anyone else but himself, and it's so tiring." Mabel said.

"Your boss is something else, can you imagine the way he just called you," she changed her voice into a baritone mimicking the caller "Um, Mabel, you're going with me to a meeting bla bla bla."

After a long pause Chika broke the silence that had existed for about three minutes. "You're going with him to that meeting," Chika said without an expression on her face.

"Babe, I have to if I still want to keep my job. I don't even have what to wear. Ha!" She walked over to the couch and stretched herself on it.

"What to wear shouldn't bother you. I have a few clothes in the closet that might just be your size, so whenever you're ready, we should check them out."

"Hmm! That works just fine." She felt a space of peace like turbulence had just been lifted off her shoulders. Chika had always been a friend since their university days. Mabel had met her when she was a year one student at the University of Port Harcourt. Chika was her roommate in the hostel and always played the role of a big sister so Mabel wouldn't get bullied by anyone. She had that thick body ever since, her curves and thick legs made people believe she was Mabel's elder sister. Since Chika graduated they've had this strong sister bond. And now they are back together as flatmates in Port Harcourt. Chika works with Mediterranean Shipping Company at 18 Trans Amadi Industrial Layout, in Port Harcourt. The pay is good and she seems to have no problem with her bosses.

Nearly five hours later, Mabel and Chika decided to check out a few clothes that would fit for the meeting. Although Chika is a size 12, she has a few clothes that are way undersized and could fit perfectly on size 10 or 11. They carefully laid dresses on the bed. Mabel tried out two of them and finally decided to go with the third option, a red sequin dress with a V-shaped neck. It stopped just below the knee and had a band at waist level, making it fit Mabel perfectly.

"This is better, ya."

"I agree."

"Madam, you can't go to such a meeting with your hair like this." Chika told her. She asked Mabel to sit while she hurriedly weaved her hair into six tight cornrows so a wig would fit. After she finished, she touched up Mabel's face with a simple makeup to enhance her beauty a bit for the evening.

"It's almost 6:00 o'clock. I need to leave, so I can meet up with my boss." The ride Mable booked took almost twenty minutes to arrive. Mabel panicked. She didn't want her boss to yell at her in public. She quickly hopped into the front passenger seat when the ride arrived.

"Hotel Presidential," she told the driver. She kept scrolling through her phone hoping and praying she would get there on time. Anyone who knows Kabiri Dan-Dagogo well enough should already know that he doesn't joke with his time. He's the most punctual person Mabel had ever met, and she wouldn't be surprised if he'd arrive at the venue about an hour before the scheduled time.

Mabel knew she was already in deep trouble with him when she got stuck in traffic. It's about that time of day when the citizens in the city go out on dates and serious night clubbing. It's a weekend, and almost all the bars had elegant men and women strolling in. It was already turning dark. The water in the tiny potholes shone in the sparkle of the awesome, yellow street lamps. The little green trees were lighted up too, as the light hit them casting significant solid shadows on them.

From a bird's-eye view, this could seem like dabs of various assortments of lights in a mix for a bouquet effect of a photograph, blazing lights—white, reds and blue—a dazzling assortment that fits together like a jigsaw puzzle, of a strong apex, painted structure. Each corner beats with activity. Fumes of stogies and cigarettes consume the space anxiously blending in with the exhaust of vehicles. Neon lights of businesses light up, appearing more splendid than Times Square. Thumping music can be heard from the nightclubs, where young people have just begun their night out. Floats of aroma, from drive-through dinners and back roads stacked with dustbins fill the air. With this smell drifting in the high sogginess, the air felt thick with a scent of hot oil and exotic food. It was an entrancing smell, giving her an energy of dangerous fire, blasting her uncovered skin like a turkey on a thanksgiving table. The deafening rambling of honks from fifty different vehicles struggling at once to beat the traffic, so they can meet up their appointment or even go back home to their wives. When the lights finally turned green, the driver rushed as fast as he could before it turned red in their lane.

Mabel was fifteen minutes late to the venue. She tried her best to meet up on time, but now she has to face her boss's wrath, after the entire meeting with the foreign investors.

Every effort to avoid being in his bad books has failed yet again.

FIVE

It was a rainy Monday morning. The downpour had begun at 6:15 a.m. One would think the taps in the sky above had been turned on by the hand of whoever makes the seasons. In a matter of seconds the whole road and neighborhood turned into a maze of small-scale streams. One could hardly accept that a couple of hours before the entire environment had been a total dry land. Water poured from the sky, darkening the morning sun that was battling to emerge until the earth couldn't drink any more, and Mabel thought the actual earth was overflowing with water too. A large portion of the trees at the other end of the compound lost a few branches after spending the last two hours bowing and ascending to the force of the yelling morning wind. Meanwhile, it continued to rain.

Mabel didn't like the weather. She was definitely going to get wet before she arrived at her office. This type of rain reminds her of her childhood experiences in Kuruama, where the children would clap and dance as the sky rumbled ready to flood the earth with rain. She and her age grades would run in the rain naked. Those older than them would wear only pants, some of which had tiny holes at the bottom. They would run round each building as the rain wiped their skin in massive strokes. Then, some of the boys would run to the town field and rub the earth mud on themselves. Childhood was fun for her, that was the only comfortable life she knew until she grew to see life from a different perspective.

Today's rain was fierce and accompanied by thunder and lightning. It had started early enough to disrupt the rest of one's day. The entire street leading to their apartment had filled with water, gushing in from left and right as the drains could no longer absorb the quantity of water released from the sky all at once. But not even the rain can stop Mabel from going to work today. She waited for the rain to sizzle down a bit, then she took off her shoes and rolled up her skirt to her thighs as she walked out of her lonely street, to the T-junction, where she could get a taxi to her workplace. It would take her thirty minutes to arrive at her office in Peter Odili Road, Trans Amadi Industrial Layout, if the road was clear from traffic.

"Trans-Amadi," she screamed loud enough so the driver could hear, as she flagged down the vehicle with her other hand. She was half wet and cold. Kabiri won't care if you're sick or dying. You have to show up at his business every single day. Every excuse made by a staff member sounded lame to him. The driver had stopped right in front of her, and she hopped into the car adjusting herself so she didn't spill water on the other passengers who were sitting beside her. By now, she was wet, almost soaked from head to toe. The road had not been too busy as some drivers prefer not to drive when it rained heavily.

The moment she got onto the company premises, she sighted her boss's car driving in right behind her. She hastily walked into the empty lobby that led to her office. She didn't recognize this as the time to exchange pleasantries with a man who is hardly ever pleased with her walking around the office.

"Ah, Mabel! Good morning." The lady who's desk was opposite hers greeted Mabel as she walked in through the door. Their office door was always left open, so people who passed by could see who was working and who was sleeping on duty. Praying is a ritual Mabel does all the time; never a day has passed that she wouldn't pray the moment she arrives at work, no matter how late she was. Other organizations that she knew go as far as conducting morning devotions, just to commit the day's activities into the hands of God, and these companies flourish in every area. TEMS Oil and Gas is a direct opposite. No one cared about praying for the well-being of the company in the morning.

Oh! Thank you, Jesus, for journey mercies. Lord, please take control of today and let every decision be ruled in my favor. Amen. She mouthed the words to her own hearing alone, but anyone who looked at her would know she was praying.

"Aunty SU" her colleague, Timi said. SU was a nickname given in high schools or universities to anyone who tries to live a Christ-like life mostly. Mabel was used to it already, since she'd given her life to Christ two years ago. She had suffered different grades of mockery from the colleagues at school, yet she didn't flinch. Some even went as far as calling her "Mary Amaka," because of the kind of clothes and skirts she wore. It wasn't as if she didn't like to look good back then; being a Christian girl doesn't mean she had to look unkempt and scraggy. She barely had enough to eat from the money her father gave her, not to talk of shopping for clothes. If not for Chika, who was always helping out, she would have suffered worse humiliation.

"I don't blame you" was all Mabel could say to her. Timi had a habit of belittling those around her. The flow of words from her mouth is capable of running down a whole car battery in a split second.

"Look, I'm not ready for your attitude this morning. I just want to mind my business here. Please leave me alone." Mabel warned her after a short pause.

"I'm sorry," Timi said, raising both hands in surrender. The main secretary watched them from the corner of her eyes.

"Thank you."

It was still muzzling outside, and Mabel wasn't comfortable with the weather. She had no place to dry herself aside from the A/C, which added more cold to her body.

She heard the composed steps of her boss made by the shoes he has on. His shoes squeaked on the tiled floor with every single step he took. She could smell him right from her office. He always wore an alluring perfume, a unique brand worn by very influential people like him, who had enough money to afford it. She quickly stopped singing to herself. His voice resonated as he scolded a staff member in the office before her's. He was definitely scolding the staff for some minor thing, she could tell from the rising and falling of his voice, but she was not near enough to hear what he was saying. He was so good at asking rhetorical questions he knew definitely would not have answers, yet he would expect you to say something at least. His footsteps were creaking in her direction—now she could hear it—yes, he was coming to her.

Her heart began to pound fast and so loudly; she could hear it. She decided to focus on her computer so that her boss would not guess that she was aware of him approaching the office. When she saw him standing by the door, she pulled herself up straighter. Her top was still wet but nicely tucked into her skirt. Kabiri Dan-Dagogo stood by the door, not unaware of the show Mabel was putting on special for him. He didn't speak until they'd all chorused, "Good morning, Sir." There was a slight pause before an answer that sounded like a groan. He took a few steps to Mabel's table and picked up the Bible she had carefully laid in front of her, turning and tossing it side to side like it was the first time he'd seen a Bible. Kate giggled at his actions and when he turned to face her, she squinted her eyes and sucked in her lower lip, swaying her broad shoulders sharply, in different directions. He took his eyes off her the moment she had started.

"What's this?" he asked after surveying the Bible like a detective.

"A-a Bible, Sir," Mabel answered haltingly. He sighed and placed the Bible back on the exact spot it had been. He traced his eyes from her head down to her toe. Too ashamed to watch him scrutinize her, she covered her feet on each other.

"Sincerely, I do not know who hired you. Take a look at your hair. You can't even keep it neat like a lady." Mabel quickly stroked the hair that had popped out from the ribbon on the other side of her head.

"It's either you're late or you're inappropriately dressed. What is WRONG with you, Mabel Sekibo?" he yelled at her. The smile that formed on Timi's face had disappeared the moment Kabiri started yelling.

"I'm sorry, Sir" Mabel whispered, her eyes faced down as much as she could. Daring to look into his face would cause a disaster for her. Tears formed in her eyes; she wiped them softly with the back of her palm. She took in a few sniffs so the liquid quickly forming in her nose would remain until he was gone at least.

"You're just despicable." He murmured and walked straight out of the office.

Mabel sobbed softly; her head rested heavily on her desk.

"Sorry o," Kate said to her mockingly, making Timi giggle with her mouth covered. This was just the first time anyone's words cut deep into her bones. The humiliation she had faced from age mates and colleagues didn't hurt as much as this does. Maybe because she had a soft spot for him and didn't expect this kind of treatment from someone she called her boss. She had felt a certain attraction for him the first day she had met him, a strange sort of feeling that made her heart skip with fear each time he was around her. The fact that she could smell the presence of this mean man, even from a distance, was not helping her situation. The only option to avert all this humiliation and torture was to quit. Yes, that was the right thing any person in his right senses would do, but this wasn't yet an option for her. She couldn't decide that. Her parents depended so much on the money she made from this job. She couldn't just quit unless she was laid off by the company. Of course, she wouldn't wish that on her enemies, only a wicked person would.

She wiped her tears. She was going to face her fears—her boss.

SIX

The last four months have been hell for Mabel. Her boss was not getting any better, and it's so obvious he is bent on relieving her of her duties.

Mabel would not stop committing every step into God's hands. She's trying her best to meet up but nothing she does seems to fit into the boss's good books and, to top it all, her supervisor, Miss Kate, would worsen the situation each time she ever decided to step in. Just the other day she had asked Mabel to create a memo for a meeting. Mable had done it perfectly to the best of her knowledge, yet Kate still picked a simple mis-spelled word she could have easily corrected. Also, the day she caught Mabel studying the Bible during lunch break, she went as far as reporting to the boss that Mabel was incompetent in her job. Two days ago, when she had reported again about some faults in the minute and report Mabel had made, Kabiri Dan-Dagogo had summoned her immediately to his office. Mabel was beginning to adjust to his daily character flares towards her, so when she got the summons, she didn't squirm as much as she would have in the past months. She knew this was the kind of person he was, a character he must have acquired as a rich man's son, with excessive pampering and spoiling from either or both of his parents. The pride sat on his shoulders like an Arabian perfume. You didn't need to be with him for a year to have a taste of his arrogance.

"Mabel," he said, "from now on, you will work under me. And just in case you don't understand, I will make it simple. You are to report directly to me from now on. I will check all the weekly reports and minutes you prepare myself. Do you understand?"

"And also," he continued with a finger pointing to the sky, "you will go with me on business meetings, every one of them," he said with a dark eye.

"Yes . . . Sir," she swallowed hard. This was her chance to prove herself, she thought. At least she would be free from her over-reacting and toxic supervisor. This new development seemed like moving from the fry pan to the fire, but she didn't care as long as she didn't have to report to a lady who hated her for no reason. Although she still had to share the same space with her, this gave her peace. After all, she wasn't answerable to her any more. Now, she had to face her nightmare.

Thursdays were always internal meetings. Mabel had sent a memo out to the various departments and posted a copy of it on the notice board in her own office. This was what she had come to see when she was first employed: that when a notice is placed on the board, it is the duty of those around to read and get the information. They all assembled in the conference room at about 2:00 p.m. This was one of those meetings where you're asked to make suggestions on how to improve the company's services.

If you ever say something reasonable, the boss would reject it. You dared not say something you think the management is doing wrong, even though you might be right. You should have prepared your resignation letter at home because you're sure not to resume the following day.

"Where's Miss Kate?" He asked, not specifically to anyone. Everyone turned their heads to different directions, and when they all noticed she was absent, Timi volunteered to look for her. A few minutes later, both Timi and Kate were back in the conference room.

"Why didn't you come along with the others?" Kabiri asked in a soft tone, his gaze fixated on Kate.

"Oh! Mabel didn't inform me about the meeting."

"You weren't informed?" He looked at Mabel with a stern look. She stared back hoping she could say it's a lie.

"Yes Sir." He didn't let her speak; he placed his palm on his head while both elbows rested heavily on the desk.

"Mabel . . ."

He opened his mouth to speak, but he let out a sigh instead.

"Shall we proceed?"

Mabel watched Kabiri speak. He had a good command of English and such a sweet accent that sometimes, one might think he has lived abroad all his life. He had only attended Abraham Lincoln University in California, but he could pass for someone who was groomed in California. Mabel took quick looks at him as he spoke, she would unconsciously let out a soft smile on her lip, silently at times.

His throaty voice was unique, she could recognize it any-where. One of the times she had stolen a glance at him, her eyes met with Kate who was watching her the way a tiger watched a bunny. She sneered down her nose at Mabel. Kate gazed intently, eyes narrowed and dripped with spite studying her with an unforgiving judgement. Kate had been instructed pri-vately by Kabiri Dan-Dagogo's girlfriend, Amina, to make sure no girl in the office had a crush on the boss, and she disliked the way Mabel looked at him sometimes. Mabel quickly looked away, focusing on her writing pad.

"Give me a copy of yesterday's report," he demanded, stretching his massive hand out to her. Mabel hurriedly searched the file and handed the requested report over to him. He read through it. The reaction on his face showed he had seen something wrong. Mabel knew he was quick at picking out errors and could embarrass anyone in front of anybody. He didn't care.

"What's this?" He queried, anger taking a hold of his dark face, his stare intense with arched brows. "You can not even spell a word as simple as reservoir, R-E-S-E-R-V-O-I-R, really?" He wheezed and threw the papers at Mabel. His action only drew a blank stare from her coworkers. But Kate wore the happiest look on her face; she couldn't hide it. She knew Mabel could not stand up to Kabiri Dan-Dagogo's girlfriend, Amina, even if she tried. The meeting ended in a really tense atmosphere. Mr. Kabiri and some of the other staff had left. After Mabel carefully packed her computer and the other typed documents into her bag, she zipped it and headed for the door. She was halfway out the door when Kate intentionally bumped into her. Mabel moved to the side creating a reasonable space for her supervisor to pass.

"I see the way you look at him. Back off. He is engaged to be married, and you don't stand a chance against the beautiful and sophisticated Amina," she whispered into Mable's ear, as she brushed shoulders with hers. Mabel almost burst out in tears, but she thought it wasn't necessary to waste her happiness on such a hateful comment. She told herself, She's literally being paid by Amina to watch for any competition with her man. That's all. Even though Mabel admired the way he speaks such fluent English, coated with such a nice choice of words, Mr. Kabiri Dan-Dagogo, from his looks, was every woman's kind of man but he hardly gives Mabel any loving looks. She must admit that, but the thought of having or nursing the idea of having a relationship with him, had never for one day crossed her mind.

The week had been a really long and stressful one. Anyone in such a stressed position would definitely crave for a serene environment, to at least clear their head. Mabel made sure she had nothing left undone before traveling to Bonny, to see her parents. She had left Port Harcourt very early on Saturday morning, since she couldn't travel after work the previous day. She needed the quietness of a serene and loving atmosphere. On her arrival, mama made pounded Yam and Banga soup with some assortments of meat and fish she had gotten from the market. Mabel saw the glow on her parents' body . At least they now had enough to eat.

"How is work?" Mama had asked.

"Hmm! Work is fine?"

"It took you so long to answer, is there a problem, my child," Mama inquired with curiosity.

Mabel took Mama down the lane of her boss and his attitude and how her supervisor thinks she has an eye for the boss and would report her to his fiancée.

"Iya!" Mama had exclaimed. "Because of a man? Hmm."

"Well, you have to be careful around her and, as to your boss, prayer is all you need. You are just being put through a test, to know how all these rich people behave at times."

"Who is in this house?"

The voice sounded familiar. Mabel knew who'd spoken from the very moment she heard the voice. Aunty Karinate had a unique high-pitched tone whenever she spoke.

"Ibote" (welcome) Mama giggled as she saw Aunty Karinate approach them in the hut.

"Aunty, Onua oh," Mabel greeted in her dialect, putting one knee on the ground, which was a sign of respect when greeting an elder.

"Iyo, Mabel, Tobira?" (How are you?)

"Ibim," (I am fine,) she answered Timidly.

Aunty Karinate rubbed Mabel on the back and pulled the seat out from the rear end of the hut to herself. Mabel knows that whenever Aunty Karinate comes to visit her parents, it was only about one thing, to report Mama's elder brother, who had suddenly turned into a drunk. All attempts to make him stop drinking the local gin have proved abortive. Mabel left the two women in the hut and headed for the beach. She had missed the smell of the sea, that salty smell that fills the atmosphere in the early hours of the evening.

Walking on the beach with a slight breeze, the cold wet sand, and the sound of the waves crashing and creating a noise that nothing can replace, Mabel took in the fresh air and stretched her arms out so she could embrace the cool breeze blowing from the ocean. The sea air had become thick with salt and humidity as it does in the evenings. She stood watching the sun set into the sea as the waves washed some seashells up onto the shore; a few of them she could recognize. She bent over and scooped a handful of the grainy sand, which looked like a million sugar grains.

"I've missed home," she said loudly. Suddenly, her phone began to ring. She quickly fumbled about in her pocket. The Caller ID read Mr. Dagogo. She let out a heavy sigh.

"Good evening, Sir," she said without hesitation.

"Evening, Mabel, how are you?"

"I'm fine."

"I have scheduled a meeting with the Lebanese expatriates tomorrow, and I want you to come along, so you can take down a few things."

She kept quiet, trying to think.

"Hello!"

"Mabel, are you there?"

"Yes Sir, but . . ." she hesitated, "I . . . I traveled to Bonny to see my parents and won't be back until tomorrow. I can't make it to the meeting, Sir."

Mr. Dagogo kept silent, but Mabel could sense the anger in the sound of his breathing over the phone. After a moment, he finally ended the call without autering a single word to her. This was so unlike her boss.

Then, Mabel panicked . . . because boats to the city don't sail until 2:00 o'clock Sundays.

SEVEN

T he new week had started off like every other week. Although Mabel was already feeling some awkward moments in the office. The day before she'd traveled, she had worked on all the files for the Bakana drilling site in Degema Local Government Area of Rivers State, Nigeria. Operations were scheduled to begin on site in two weeks. This project meant a lot to the company and after the last meeting, all staff of TEMS Oil and Gas had been admonished to put hands on deck, so that operations with the Lebanese on the site would go on smoothly. Mabel made sure everything was in place and tried her best to meet up with standards. At least with the rigorous training and yelling from her boss within the short time she has worked with him, she now has some experience, even though he still yelled at her at the slightest opportunity. What had kept her going was an old adage that her mother used to say back in the village: "Something you do not have any knowledge of is bigger than you."

Mabel was aware she was not as experienced as the others in the field, but the quest for more knowledge has made her swallow all the insults and humiliation from her boss. In this short period, she's met a lot of influential people in the society, people her own supervisor has yet to meet. Mr. Kabiri Dan-Dagogo is still angry that she'd traveled and didn't meet up for the meeting with the Lebanese the other day. The whole week has been him reminding her of how unserious she is about her job.

The meeting with the Bakana chiefs was conducted successfully. Except for Mabel, who was just a new staff member, only the very senior staff of the company were present in the meeting. This time she comported herself and professionally managed her space, to avoid the malicious looks she had received from Kate in the previous meetings. She made sure her writings and spellings were checked; it won't be funny if her boss embarrassed her in front of these titled men. She could take in the vicious scolding in front of her colleagues, but with these men, it would be a suicidal trip for her. The meeting ended on a good note. Mabel returned to her office. A few minutes after she settled in, Mr. Kabiri called her on the phone. She began packing her stuff into her bag, one item after the other.

"Where are you going?" Timi asked.

"The MD says I have to go with him to the state government house right now." Mabel replied.

From the other side of the office, where she had her desk, Kate flashed her a scornful look. She rolled her eyes up and down at Mabel, who just walked away after letting her know she was closed for the day. She'd heard Kate snap her fingers at her. The kind of snap that depicts dealing severally with someone who is getting on your nerves, or someone who has offended you.

By the time Mable finished with her boss, she was entirely exhausted. When she eventually got home at 7:00 p.m. she didn't take off her office clothes. She didn't see any reason to wait a minute without rushing into the kitchen to get food. She brought out a plate of chicken stew from the freezer and put it in the sink to thaw, then she cut out a portion enough for her and Chika to eat for the night. She quickly poured it into a bowl and pushed it into the microwave. It wasn't completely frozen, so it would only take a couple of minutes to get heated. She also put some rice on the fire to boil while she took her bag and shoes to her room and prepared to get a shower. From her room she heard the chime from the doorbell.

"Who's there?" She asked as she walked towards the door.

Mabel greeted her flatmate, "Oh! Chika, you're welcome," she says.

"Thank you, Sis."

"Why didn't you use your keys?"

"Babe, I forget them in the morning while hurrying out for work."

"Oh okay, I want to bathe; there's rice on the fire, so you can take a bath as well, then come out for dinner, ya!"

Chika nodded and went into her room. After Mabel had finished bathing, she went to the kitchen and sorted out the food for the both of them. She pulled out two plates from the kitchen drawer and served out rice for each person from the pot. Each of the plates had a nicely seasoned piece of chicken in it. She placed both plates on the small dining table, and the two ladies enjoyed their dinner quietly.

It had been two months since the last meeting was held by the Degema Council of Chiefs concerning the drilling site in their community. TEMS Oil and Gas had been asked to award at least a hundred scholarship slots to indigenous members of the community who were in higher institutions of learning, whether male or female. The agreement had been signed by the Council of Chiefs and the company, and it was to take effect within four weeks. All documents were signed and handed to both parties.

"Mabel, please come forward with the agreement file for the Degema drilling site, and send a copy to my mail," her boss told her over the telephone.

"Okay, Sir."

She quickly got on her system and searched the file name on her search bar but it didn't pop up like it should have, if the file was stored on her computer. So she took her time to check out the files, one after the other. When she still couldn't find the agreement file for the Degema drilling site she became nervous.

"Are you looking for something?" Timi had asked her.

"Yes," Mabel responded with a straight face. The document was too important to the company and to her. If it has gone missing, she definitely wouldn't want to know her fate. She pulled out the side drawer attached to her table and combed through every single document in it. There was a fierce rustling sound as she carefully placed them, one after the other on her desk.

"Ah! Ah!" Mabel exclaimed in confusion.

"But I left it here in my drawer," she said almost to herself.

The whirring sound from the telephone on her desk got her almost jumping out of her skin. She picked up the receiver and placed it to her ear.

"Mabel, don't keep me waiting," the boss's voice roared from the other end of the phone.

"O . . . okay, Sir," she stammered and placed down the receiver.

"What are you searching for with so much energy?" Kate asked.

"Miss Kate, I am looking for the Degema agreement file I kept in my drawer. I can't find it."

"Wow! You can't find it?" Kate asked in surprise. "You can reprint one from your system, can't you?"

"Yes . . . ," a pause. "The thing is that I can't find it on my system either."

Kate didn't reply to her last sentence. Instead, she went out the door and straight to the boss's office to report. A few minutes after, she was back in the office, with her face looking like a little demon coated in ash.

"The MD wants you in his office right away," she said with a malicious glee.

"Okay," Mabel muttered furiously under her breath.

Mabel's heart began to pound so loudly she could hear it; she feared if she attempted to say a single word her heart would fall out of her mouth.

"Jesus, I need Your help right now," she kept whispering to herself as she walked behind her supervisor.

"Sir," Mabel said as she stood in front of the boss.

He cleared his throat.

"Kate told me you've misplaced the document I asked you to keep."

"Sir,"

"I don't want to hear anything from you."

Suddenly, Kate barged in "Sir, I have told you times without number that this lady here is incompetent and careless. I have to pick up files from our office floor almost every single day, when she has closed for the day. This same file, I have warned her times without number to scan and save it to the other document files on her computer, but she wouldn't listen. Now you see?"

"Uhm! Kate, leave us. please . . .."

"Alright, Sir," she said and left, making sure she quacked her shoulders against Mabel's on her way to the door.

"Come, sit," he beckoned calmly and brought out a paper from his drawer.

"I have tried to manage you for months. I even made sure you worked directly with me, so you could learn the ethics of this job. But it's now obvious you do not want to help yourself. For your information, this company cannot afford to place you on any training whatsoever. We do not have that kind of money and time to waste on someone as incompetent as you, Mabel."

Mabel's hands trembled. Her entire body shook vigorously as tears began to dampen her eyes. Kabiri pushed a pink paper to her and placed a pen on it. "Tender your resignation," he said softly.

"Sir, please . . . see,"

He didn't care.

"I am being kind enough by giving you a chance to tender your resignation yourself. Do not force me to shove a sack letter in your face. Young lady, sign the damn paper and get the hell out of my office." He barked the order at her. She hesitated then went down on her knees pleading and begging.

He picked up the receiver and punched in some numbers.

"Security, there's a young lady in my office I want you to see off these premises."

"Come NOW, my friend!" he barked into the receiver.

EIGHT

M abel cried all the way down to her office. Some of the staff who had seen her walk as slowly as a wet cat into her office had asked her what the problem was, but she obviously didn't give an answer.

"Who died?" One had asked with care. He stood watching her in utmost confusion as she drifted, wiping her tears with the back of her palm repeatedly. When she got to her office she stood by the door for a few minutes and surveyed the room like she hadn't seen it before. Two years of hard work and dedication gone without compensation whatsoever. She had tried to explain to him but Kabiri wasn't the type of man who would budge on his decisions, even for a second. Tears streamed down her eyes uncomfortably as she walked to her seat.

"What happened?" Timi panicked. Her curiosity covered her face like a deep Harmattan dust cloud. Mabel didn't respond, instead she pushed the paper in front of her. Timi picked it up, her hands shaking as she read through the letter word for word.

"Heeey! How did this happen?" She asked, feeling more sorry than happy.

"This is so bad."

"Thank you." Mabel said as she retrieved the letter from her. She carefully folded it into her bag then arranged her things, which no longer belonged to her, on the desk.

"Timi, please help me return this laptop to my boss." She said as she sniffed one more time. Her eyes were puffed and accompanied with a greasy red nose. She turned to face Kate who had a slightly softened expression and the faintest hint of a smile playing at the corner of her lips.

"Don't worry, you'll get another job," she said, playing with the keys she has in her hand.

Thirty minutes after Mabel left the company premises, Amina showed up. First, she went in to see her fiancé who was already having a bad day. Those files were important to him; his company was at stake. The Degema Council of Chiefs could sue him for trespassing.

"Oh my God," he said, rubbing his hand on his nicely cut hair.

"Knock, knock" sounds as the door is pushed open with a hard shove.

"Hey, Babe, are you okay?" she asked, casually flinging her bag on his desk.

"It's nothing. I will be fine" he responded, attempting to fake a smile and then stopped right the moment he had attempted it.

"Wait, is it because of Mabel?"

"I beg your pardon?"

"You're moody, Kabiri, and I need to know why, so I ask again, is Mabel the reason for your mood?"

"No, no way? How could you even think of something as ridiculous as that?" He asked, adjusting himself on his seat. "She'd misplaced an important document, so I fired her."

"She's incompetent and I wouldn't be needing her around here anymore" he said, rubbing his eyes with the tip of his middle finger. Amina moved closer, setting half of her butt on his desk while her legs hung suspended in the air like some monkey stuck on a tree. She cupped his face with her hands and gently stroked his soft whiskers. He scrunched his face up a little and flashed her a smile similar to a smirk. His stare was blank and unreadable.

"You need to calm down," she said as she leaned over and pressed a soft kiss on his head.

"I need to see Kate," she informed him.

"Which Kate?" he asked with so much curiosity in his eyes.

"Your secretary," she sniggered.

"What for?"

"Well, girls' stuff," she said as she twirled left and right.

"I'll be right back, Hun," she said and blew him an invisible kiss with her lips pout on her right palm. Kabiri leaned back in his seat the moment Amina closed the door behind her.

She swayed her hips swiftly, taking slow but elegant steps as she strolled down the hallway to Kate's office. The moment she was at the door, she paused to smooth her hair like a model on parade. She walked slowly into the office exposing the straight legs in her high-heeled shoes.

"Hi, Kate," she said standing directly in front of her. Kate jilted a bit and raised her head to catch a better sight of Amina.

"Ah! My friend, you are welcome." She let out a short laugh that seemed not to go down her throat. Timi walked in just then. Shocked to see Amina in their office instead of the boss, she wondered what kind of relationship the duo had to make Amina of all people stoop below her class to visit their office today.

"Good morning, Ms. Amina," Timi said.

"Thank you," Amina responded casually without turning for a second.

"Meet me in my car," she said to Kate almost in a whisper.

"Sure," Kate responded. She stood up from her seat almost immediately following behind Amina. Timi watched them until they were out of sight. Whatever business they had going on wasn't pure Timi thought in her heart.

"I heard you've done a good job with the snitch." Amina spoke the minute they were both seated in her car.

"Yes, the boss fired her just an hour ago. She's gone for good," Kate said as she laughed out loud.

Amina let out a soft groan.

"You know," Kate continued. "She didn't only have eyes for the boss, she was desperately after my position."

Amina said, "I guess we are both free from her spell then?"

"Yes, we are," and they both laughed.

"Well, I sent in some money a few days ago," Amina said.

"I received it," Kate put in sharply.

"Alright, I will make a transfer of ₦800,000 to your account right away for a job well done." Amina picked up her phone.

"Really?"

"Yes, just hold on."

It didn't take three minutes before Kate had a whooping ₦800,000 sitting pretty in her bank account.

"Hey, thank you," she said.

"No, I should be thanking you for getting rid of the parasite so easily. You can return the file to him in a few weeks or days."

"Alright, see you some other time, and don't forget to keep an eye on my man." Amina ended the conversation.

"Sure, I will." Kate said and got out of the car. She smiled all the way back to her office. The money was huge for a task as simple as getting rid of some imposter. But she was still going to take her own shot at the boss. A selfish woman like Amina shouldn't be in the boss's good book. She thought.

"Anyways good riddance to bad rubbish." She mouthed.

Back in her office Kate took a file from the drawer and studied it for a while.

"Yes."

She adjusted her blouse, exposing a good part of her cleavage. She ran her hand on her silk hair and zoomed off to the CEO's office.

"Knock, knock."

Then she pulled the knob slowly. When she got in, Kabiri had his eyes fixed on the door wondering *Who is it this time? He didn't need any disturbance at this point.*

"Yes, Kate. What is it?" He asked shifting his focus immediately on his computer.

"Uhm, Sir," she said, her skirt resting perfectly on her soft thighs. "You have an appointment with the new site engineers at 2:00 p.m. today."

"Cancel it."

"What?"

"You heard me, Kate." He barked.

"I'm sorry, Sir."

She moved closer a bit, so he could get a better view of the exposed flesh popping out from the opening in her beautiful satin top.

"Here's the file, Sir. All appointments for today are in it."

"Cancel them all," he said as he gave her a dangerous look. "And you can place the file on the last cabinet over there," he told her pointing to the other end of the office. Kate walked swaying her hips in an unconventional way; she's got a perfect back side, the type every typical Efik woman would have. He kept his eyes fixed on her.

When she got to the shelf he'd indicated she slowly bent over in a sweetly seductive way. Her butt stuck out as though it would burst open from the short skirt.

"Kate, put the file down and leave my office at once." He said softly. When she hesitated, he walked over to her, held her by the arm and pushed her out.

What did he do wrong with these women these days he wondered to himself. He was confused, thinking What's wrong with these women these days? Do they even have shame?

Flirting with a staff member was something Kabiri wasn't going to do. Some of his colleagues did and most times it didn't turn out good at the end. Mixing work and love is strictly against work ethics. He knew this was an important issue he would have to tackle, but first he has to address the problem at hand.

"What nonsense!" He snorted.

He took off his jacket and rested himself heavily on his seat. He picked up a little towel and dabbed his now sweaty palms.

He continued swiveling.

NINE

Mabel had been fighting the feeling of letting her parents know about her dismissal from work. They both depended on her so much that she split her salary into two for their monthly upkeep since she was all they've got. She had been in her room all day as nothing seemed to interest her anymore. She only made time to go through the three weeks online course she had enrolled for. She had finished the last part and had applied to the job post Chika had forwarded to her on WhatsApp a few days ago. Thinking about the years she spent working for TEMS—the time, energy, and resources—all she could do was cry. And now, the little allowance she got during the out-of-work-time meetings won't be coming in anymore.

"Mabel, crying every day will not help the situation here, and you can't tell Mama and Papa about this." Chika said, interrupting her thoughts. Chika had sneaked in without her notice.

"You know how heartbreaking this will be to them. You applied to the job post I sent you a week ago, right? Obinna holds a big position in that company." She continued and sat on the bed.

"Obinna . . .which Obinna?" Mabel asked, wiping her tears. She looked more interested than she had been because getting a good job in Port Harcourt these days required the grace of God and having a strong person at the top who could help you.

"The Student Christian Fellowship president back then in school. You were new then, so I understand if you don't know him."

"You know what hurts me the most? The fact that I don't know how that document got missing . . . I can't explain what happened. I packed them up myself into that drawer. What really amazes me is how the same document disappeared from my computer. I saved it myself and no one shares the computer with me. That document is important to that company. Kabiri might lose everything he's worked for."

"Uhm! That's his loss and not yours. One quality of a good boss that I know is the ability to listen to his workers, and if he can't give that, then, Sis, he isn't worth your tears. Okay, cheer up."

"I will put in a call for you. Anything for a sister," Chika said and gave Mabel a hug.

"And you know, the best revenge to give Mr. Dagogo is to get a better position at REN Petroleum Company. It's a fast-growing firm, and from all indications, it beats TEMS at all levels. So keep your fingers crossed my dear. A single call will do the job."

Rushing through the bustling streets of Port Harcourt, Mabel hurriedly walked as fast as her legs could carry her down to the park where she could take a taxi to her interview. Since she left TEMS Oil and Gas she had prayerfully waited for a sweet day like this. The advert in Punch newspaper didn't contain much criteria for the job. Her two years working with Kabiri Dan-Dagogo has taught her a lot of things she could build on with this new job. This was God giving me another chance to prove myself. She had thought to herself when the interview invite popped in her mail three weeks after she'd applied for the position of a secretary. Only a fool will not step up her game after all the rigorous training with Kabiri.

She arrived at REN Petroleum Company thirty minutes before the scheduled time for the interview. This is one of the fastest growing companies in Port Harcourt. It has a very large building. Anyone who worked here was believed to be a big boy in town. When she approached the sliding door, it opened automatically, the moment she stepped close. She walked in straight to the reception and took her seat. Just then, a beautifully dressed dark lady came out from one of the rooms and gave her a warm welcome. Others were seated too. She was nervous but still managed to keep her cool.

It didn't take long before she found the man's office door. She muttered a short prayer to herself before knocking on the door three times.

"Come in" she heard him say cheerfully.

Mabel stepped inside with a smile.

"Hi, Ms. Sekibo, please have a seat." The man in front of her said. He was a man of about forty years, tall and fine, and he seemed to have a good sense of humor.

"Ms. Sekibo," he said sternly, waiting for her to reply. She didn't even realize he had asked her something.

"Let's start. What experience do you have in working, Ms. Sekibo?"

Mabel paused, then she told him, "I had Worked with TEMS Oil and Gas for two years."

"Wait," he said, "You've worked with TEMS?"

"Yes."

"That means you know Mr. Kabiri Dan-Dagogo?"

"Yes. I do. He was my boss and I worked directly under his supervision."

"Hmm. Interesting. From your CV I can see that you're a graduate of Mass Communication."

"You're right, Sir."

"So, why aren't you working in a TV or Radio station?" He asked and, for unknown reasons he didn't let Mabel answer.

"Never mind, Ms. Sekibo. Tell me why you want us to hire you?"

"Well, I want to work in a challenging environment where I can harness my skills and direct them majorly to the growth of the company." She offered.

He didn't say a word after Mabel's response. He paused for a while then scribbled a note she could not see into a black diary. He asked her a series of questions like her age, why she left her other job, how she is right for this job, and a host of others. He also told a bit of what the job is about and what she would be doing as the head secretary. Shortly after, he said she should wait in the reception while he and his team discussed her application. She wondered a little at this odd request, then thanked him and stepped out into the waiting room.

It didn't take long before she was called into his office again. "Have a seat, Ms. Sekibo, he said the moment she got into his office.

"Well, we've decided to hire you as the new Head of Operations. The previous one resigned last month and has traveled overseas with his family. Our company is fast growing, and if we are impressed by your skills and dedication to your work you'll get a raise in position and salary. Em, we want the best for all our staff, so we try as much as we can to make them very comfortable while working with us."

These words made Mabel smile from ear to ear. "That was fast," she said.

"Yes, I know and it is very unusual for our company to hire within a day, but your CV says much and a good friend of mine put in a few good words for you. Also, we've taken into consideration the fact that you've worked with Mr. Kabiri Dan-Dagogo, a gem in the industry for two solid years. We believe that you will impart what you've learnt there into our system."

"Congratulations," he said as he stretched out his hand for a handshake. Mabel took his hand in hers and gave a warm grip. Then he handed the appointment letter to her.

"Thank you so much, Sir." she said.

"You will resume next week. We are giving you this week off, so you can put yourself together. If that works for you?"

"Yeah. Sure it does." She quickly read through the appointment letter. The position has a huge salary, a company car, clothes allowance, and a house in the GRA phase 2. She smiled widely.

"Do you like what you see, Ms. Sekibo?"

"Yes I do and it's far above my expectations, Sir."

"You might need some driving lessons, if you can't already drive."

Mabel nodded her head vigorously in agreement. She thanked him and dipped the appointment letter into her bag. She headed home so happily. She couldn't wait to get home before breaking the good news to Chika.

She dialed Chika's number as she stepped into a taxi home.

"Guess what?" she said with excitement in her voice.

"You got the job?"

"Yes, I did. And the pay is HUGE." She screamed into the phone. "It comes with a lot of bonuses, a house, a car, and monthly wardrobe allowance."

"Oh, congratulations, Baby! I'm so happy for you. Thank God; I'm so happy it worked out just nice."

"We will celebrate when I get home, okay? Be safe," Mabel said and hung up. She placed the phone on her chest and placed her head on the head rest at the back seat.

This was the best news she had received in recent days. Staying at home and doing absolutely nothing most of the time, had helped her to trust God, and she couldn't help thinking, This can only be God's doing. And to Chika she will forever be grateful.

She went home smiling from ear to ear. Unbelievable, a house in the New GRA phase 2? Everyone living in Port Harcourt knew that GRA is for big government officials and respected multinational oil expatriates.

She danced and praised God in songs while preparing the Egusi soup she had planned on making in the evening before she received the call from REN Petroleum Company. The air in the company felt chilling and welcoming the very moment she stepped in. Even the staff she met had smiles all over their faces but she vows to be extremely careful with both colleagues and her documents because, once bitten twice shy. Bad history mustn't repeat itself.

TEN

It had been a month since Mabel hade left TEMS Oil and Gas. Even though Kabiri Dan- Dagogo had complained of her being incompetent, lately he missed yelling at her. He missed working with her and, for some unexplainable reason, he knew deep down Mabel was a kind person, the type of woman who never complained for the bad treatments; unlike Kate, who hissed and frowned when things weren't going her way.

Things are just not the same any more.

Sitting in his office on this hot afternoon. Kabiri Dan-Dagogo has his jacket resting on one arm of the chair.

Kabiri picked up the receiver and dialed Kate's office. He had wanted her to help send an email to the expatriates in China, since he'd be having a Zoom meeting with them in a couple of hours. "Kate, I called you thirty minutes ago and you have yet to show up at my office. Come at once!"

This was one of the reasons he missed Mabel. There'd never been a day he'd called her and she hesitated. She always had a way of running down to his office in a split second. But he wondered about the uncomfortable times she had to go on diverse off-hours meetings with him.

Kabiri let out a big sigh. Definitely, he knows that he cannot find anyone good enough to replace Mabel's enthusiasm for the effortless work. Now, he's forced to work with this crazy lady he calls his secretary. The deed has been done, and calling

Mabel back will be a defeat on his part, he wasn't going to let that happen.

"Sir, you called," Kate said as she opened the door to his office.

"I called you about thirty minutes ago. Look at the time you showed up, yet you complained months ago about how incompetent and lazy Mabel was. Your performance in terms of punctuality is worse than Mabel's, and if you're not careful you will leave me with no other option but to fire you." He scolded Kate with his finger pointed at her.

"Yes . . . , Boss." She responded.

He continued to scroll through his laptop while she went out to her office forwarding the mail as he had directed her.

Wait a minute. I hope this isn't what I'm thinking, he thought in his heart. All the messages he had forwarded to the business partners from the Delta had not been delivered on the chat since yesterday. "What could be the problem?" he said softly. He tried sending another enquiry, and when it still didn't deliver he picked up his phone and dialed their contact.

He dialed Feghor on his mobile phone . . .

"What do you mean, it's not reachable?" Huh?

He scrolled through his phone and dialed Raphael's number; it still isn't reachable. He ran his hand over his head and, even though the A/C was on, a tiny sheen of sweat began to form on his forehead. Mabel had tried to warn him about these guys on the very night he fixed a meeting with them.

"Sir, I have a feeling these men are only out to dupe you," she had said.

"Mabel, in this business we don't deal with feelings. Your feelings won't put food on my table," he had responded to her.

He quickly waved the memory out of his mind as he paced back and forth in his office. The sudden ringing of his phone interrupted his thought. He walked hastily to the table and picked up the phone.

"Hello, Tega."

"Boss," Tega greets him from the other end of the phone.

"Yes, Tega, em . . . , I've been trying to reach Feghor and Raphael for some time, but both numbers aren't connecting."

"Em, Sir, there's been some trouble at the site. We tried working on site this morning and some men came to say we must leave the site. And, when we asked why, they called us thieves and intruders and they attacked us. They've arrested several of the other engineers, but I managed to escape."

"What do you mean, they called you intruders. I paid for drilling on that site. I spent a whooping sum of ₦70,000,000, for drilling on that site. I signed the papers myself. So, what's the problem now?"

"Boss, I think you've been duped. The guys you signed with aren't the real owners, Sir. Kindly go to the police station and make a statement, so the other engineers can be released."

"What station are they being held at?"

"Ozoro police station, Sir."

"Whoo!" He inhaled and exhaled, "Okay. I will send an order for their release immediately."

The call ended.

The door opened sharply and Kabiri turned around to find Amina standing beside him.

"Hey, there," his face wasn't as bright as the usual times she'd visited him at work.

"Hey. Aren't you happy to see me, Baby?"

"It's not that," he said, giving her a short kiss on the cheek. He held her at arm's length and surveyed her for a while before saying, "You look good though."

"Thank you," she said, blushing. She thought in her heart that nothing would be as soothing to her, right now than the compliments coming from her own man, Kabiri Dan-Dagogo.

"So, what's up with you? You don't look fine to me?"

"You know," I just lost some huge amount of money to some dupes I thought were my trusted business associates." He signed heavily.

"I'm so sorry, Love. Let's do dinner tonight?"

"Eem . . . I think I have a meeting set at 7:30 p.m. today."

"Very well then. We'll go to the meeting together, after dinner."

"Okay." He said softly.

"I think l have to close for the day; it's almost 4:00 p.m." Just then, there was a soft knock on his door, and Kate walked in in her usual seductive manner with her skirt pulled high up to her thighs and her cleavage exposing so much skin on her chest.

She quickly adjusted herself the moment she walked in and found Amina in Kabiri's office. Kate stuttered, "Good . . . E-evening, Ma'am." She said with her eyes down on her toes. She kept pulling her skirt down as she spoke and tried to subtly adjust her chiffon top to cover her cleavage.

Amina flashed her a harsh and unforgiving look, sharp enough to tear her flesh into shreds. Kate quickly recoiled into her shell like a tortoise poked on the head with a sharp object.

Kabiri broke the awkward silence, "Em . . . , Kate?"

"Sir?"

"I will be going to the meeting with Amina, so do not bother anymore." He said holding Amina closer to himself without looking at Kate. Amina stroked his beard softly with her middle finger, while her eyes focused on Kate, who was now raining curses in her mind.

"Okay, Sir" she responded after a long pause and turned to leave.

"You came in to say something?"

"It's not important, Sir. I can sort it out myself."

"Alright then, see you tomorrow. You can cancel all the other meetings and fix the other clients today. I can't afford to lose these contracts with the Lebanese investors."

"Okay, Sir," she answered and wiggled her way out of the office.

"Is she alright?" Amina asked.

"I don't know. Why?"

"She's acting weird around you; can't you see it?"

"Well, I can't, Madam. The only person I see here is you."

"Shall we leave already?"

"Sure, why not."

On their way out, Amina excused herself and secretly went to Kate's office.

"Bitch, I see how you act around him." She let out a short crooked laugh.

"Your job is to watch him and not flirt with him."

"I'm trying my best, but since Mabel left you haven't given me any attention."

"You will, soon enough, just be a good girl" Amina patted Kate repeatedly on her back and left.

Kate held her hand to her chest as she watched Amina leave the office. Thank God Timi isn't in at the moment. Kate quickly walked to the door and peered around the edge of the frame to check if anyone had eavesdropped on their conversation.

"Thank Goodness, nobody heard." She said as she took a deep breath and walked back to her seat.

As much as Kate's working as a watchdog for Amina, she wants Kabiri for herself. He's tall, dark, handsome, and wealthy, a sure spec for every woman. Men like Kabiri have women flocking around them, but will most likely settle for a woman in their class and social status or at least someone close. Amina is a senator's daughter, and Kate can't possibly win a competition with her. Kate knows this, yet she's chosen to keep hitting hard on an impossible mission.

Her plan is to make him look her way.

ELEVEN

The last two weeks have been really tough on Kabiri. He had always made mistakes, but none of them has resulted in foolishness. First, it was a whooping seventy million naira dupe from men he thought were his business associates.. The loss was definitely going to hit hard if not properly handled. Until this incident, he had never had any thought about inviting external auditors, but things are beginning to drift.

It seemed like the walls holding the company were beginning to crack. He hadn't thought about it until it was time to fund the scholarship scheme he had signed for undergraduates in Degema. Even though he hadn't been able to understand the mystery behind the missing documents file, he had gone ahead to create a new one. Since then at least hundred undergraduates from Degema had enjoyed a sum of one hundred thousand naira each as bursary payments for the past year.

This year wasn't going to be different and, in order to maintain the peace at the drilling site, all contract terms must be met. Kate had been the replacement for Mabel since she'd left and had been handling a few transactions from some of the meetings.

Kabiri didn't trust the accounting that much, and since he had worked with Mabel without worrying about missing funds, he doesn't see any reason for not giving Kate the same honor of handling a few official transactions. Meetings as big as those always end with tips. Kate enjoyed every bit of her out-of-work-time meetings, until Amina decided to show up, ruining every single plan Kate had made for herself. Though the boss didn't look her way, he had never for one day denied her the tip that she deserved for working the extra hours. Sometimes, she had to take notes and draft out minutes she knew for sure would not be used in the future. The shocking thing to her was that Amina has forgotten so soon how she had helped her keep an eye on Kabiri. She's the one to spend the entire day with the boss whenever he is around, so looking good isn't a bad idea, or just maybe she had dragged Mabel too soon.

All extra stipends have been stopped since she no longer goes on those meetings and, to worsen the entire situation, Amina always shows up unannounced, then she would work in his office like she owned 95 percent of it. She would always bark orders at staff and expect them to respond "a s a p." It's one thing to have a grumpy boss and another to have an overly protective girlfriend who would show up at his multinational company uninvited, just to watch who has an eye for her fiancé. On some occasions, Amina would bring him lunch, some of which he never touched.

Like every organization, accountants were hired by TEMS to conduct audits just so everything could be put to check from finances to expenses and profits. The audit had announced the money available in the company account for all expenses, was for a period of four months, instead of six, which had always been updated within two halves of the year.

After the first five months of work, external auditors were invited to conduct a strictly independent assessment of the company's financial statements and disclosures to ensure that there were no fraudulent activities or material misstatements. This is because there has not been any auditing during the past eight months.

When the accountants openly announced that there weren't enough funds for the Degema Student Bursary, it came as a shock to the entire staff who were present at the meeting.

"What do you mean, there aren't enough funds? This company makes way above fifty million naira on a monthly basis, apart from the extra money that comes as profit from the foreign investors?" Something wasn't right and he knew it.

"External auditors will be coming next week," Kabiri announced. Maybe, all of these shortages and no funds bullshit will be sorted out."

After he was done with the meeting, Kabiri retired to his office and, while he rocked himself on his seat trying to figure out what was the main reason for the losses, Amina came in with two packs of Chinese food she'd ordered on her way to his office.

"Hey, Babe, look what I got." She said as she raised the brown bag pack to her face. She walked closer to where he was seated and pecked him on his left cheek. He gave her a smile akin to a smirk.

"What's it, you don't like it?" she asked.

"I do. I'm glad you got it."

"Okay . . . so what are you up to?"

"Just work stuff," he said.

"Look at you. You're pale and you've got eye bags. You need a rest, Sweetheart."

"You know I can't rest, Amina. Telling me to rest from a business that puts food on my table is like telling me not to breathe anymore."

"Oh!" She bluffed.

She knew she wasn't going to win the argument with him just like she had never done, whenever he was in a mood such as this. He turned to her and said, "I know. I don't know if this feeling is right, but do you know since Mabel left, I have been battling with guilt, and business hasn't been too good?"

"Wait, same old Mabel?" Amina asked.

"The incompetent secretary?" she said.

Amina helped him unbox the food and both began eating. The external auditors came in a bit earlier than expected. The entire staff were on a stampede. The next two days had been scheduled for rigorous audits and checks. All heads of departments had sent their reports.

A few hours after going through all the financial records and reviews presented, the senior auditor, Mrs. Miebaka, asked the accountant a few quick questions which she believed gave accurate figures with what he calculated but the statements from the bank and the documents presented from the transactions, showed that there was a huge amount of money missing from the organisation's accounts, and this theft could not be a crime performed by just one person.

Kate hadn't liked the idea of bringing in external auditors. She had tried several times to convince Kabiri to shift the audit till the end of the year, claiming that would be the best time to sort out any mismanagement. After the meeting, Mr. Kabiri invited the head auditor into his office. He expressed his frustration as much as he could.

"What do you suggest I do, Mrs. Miebaka?"

She paused and watched him for a second as though thinking of the perfect answer to give him before she spoke, "Like I said earlier," she began, "there's been a lot of theft going on underground for the past one year and four months, going by the records. The figures presented did not tally with what we found out to be the gross income for six months. Money has been moving for the past months right into an account, which my team and I would need a few days to track and examine."

"Okay, then I will leave you to do your thing, but please let me know if you need anything at all."

"Umm, Mr. Kabiri, and there's one more thing.

"We realized you also have a bad spending habit, and you are part of the reasons for this loss because your expenses are way above your income and if you continue this way you will surely go bankrupt or fall deeply into debt. I am sure you do not want that, Mr. Kabiri?"

"Of course not," he responded firmly.

"I beg to take my leave," Mrs. Miebaka said. "Whatever comes up, I shall relate it to you personally."

"Thank you, Mrs. Miebaka," he said and shook her hand before seeing her off to the door.

"Arrr!" He paced the room to and fro, not exactly looking for something but he had his eyes running over almost all the objects in his office. He finally paused by his window with his hands in his pockets. His heart raced fast.

This was entirely his fault. Kabiri knows he has been too strict on these workers and they naturally want to pay him back. His father had built this company from scratch; he had worked tirelessly to make sure his son got a legacy.

From the records he had carefully checked since he became the MD, there hadn't been any form of theft or mismanagement. TEMS had never begged anyone for assistance, and it won't start in my time he thought within himself. He shook the thought out of his head. His father had warned him of his spending habits before his demise. Kabiri didn't need a seer to tell him all wasn't well. "Whatever has to do, must be done, and very fast." He said in a whisper, pointing out his little finger as though he had figures written down on a blackboard.

Kabiri moved his finger in the air from the first invisible figure to the second. He didn't stop. He sighed, taking off his suit jacket. He drew out his handkerchief from his jacket's breast pocket and wiped off the tiny beads of sweat forming on his forehead.

"Anyone involved, will pay dearly," he said.

TWELVE

The second day of the audit began as calmly as the very first day had. No one ever expected the outcome, until names of a few staff, who had been associated with certain fraudulent activities and massive financial mismanagement of company funds, were called.

TEMS Oil and Gas was said to be facing turbulent times at this moment, which was very unusual. Nevertheless, the board had decided that, whatever the source of the failure in the system was, it must be corrected immediately, before things got out of hand.

Following the closed meeting Kabiri Dan-Dagogo had with the head auditor, he was ready for the worst that could happen with his employees, as none of them was to be trusted at this point in time. The atmosphere at TEMS Oil and Gas was tense, and productive activity was at a standstill. Every staff member walked and talked with caution, just to avoid getting into the boss's bad book.

The morning had begun on an awkward note. Kabiri could no longer understand what was going on in his establishment.

He drove into the premises at about 7:30 a.m., which was quite early for him. He still maintained a gorgeous look, just like he had always done, before all the troubles started.

He walked past a few staff in the hallway leading to his office and couldn't recall giving a response to their greetings. His mind was fixed, and he was determined to get to the root of all this financial trouble.

When he got to his office, he slotted the key into the keyhole and turned it twice, till it opened. He then stepped into his office like a king. This was a strange feeling for him because, for the last ten years, he usually had his office cleaned up and opened before he arrived at work each day. That was how long he had worked as the CEO of this company. His father had willed it to him.

He took a deep breath and ran his fingers over his perfectly pressed shirt and through his nicely cut hair. His eyes caught the framed picture of his late father hanging on the wall. He walked closer to it and stared for a while.

"I'm so sorry, Father," he began. "Running a business such as this is hectic. I have tried all I could, and things still aren't going the right way, like they would have if you were here. I miss you, Dad, and I wish all of this would just stop, 'cause I'm losing my mind."

He had just finished his soliloquy when he heard a knock on his door.

"Come in," he said, grumbling the words out of his throat, like he had a stone in his esophagus. The door flung open at his response. He turned around and found Mrs. Miebaka standing behind him.

"Good morning, Mr. Kabiri."

"Mrs. Miebaka, good morning,' he responded calmly.

"Well, my team and I are ready for today's task, and your staff are also sitting right now in the conference room, so I thought to inform you myself."

Taking control of the moment, Kabiri said, "Thank you so much for your concern, Ma'am. I will be with you shortly."

"Okay, then. We will be waiting."

Mrs. Miebaka left his office shortly after ensuring that he would be present at the meeting.

Kabiri wasn't sure of the outcome of the meeting; however he was optimistic that the external auditors would do their job effectively. At least, he'd worked with Mrs. Miebaka for some years and he was certain about her credibility. She was his father's closet ally and wanted the best for the firm too.

Kabiri strolled slowly into the conference room. Kate, Mr. Jones the accountant, Mr. Spiff the regional head of operations, and the heads of the major departments of the firm were all seated.

He pulled out his seat and sank himself in it without looking at anyone in particular.

"Shall we begin," he said, flipping through the documents that had been placed on his table before him.

The chief auditor, Mrs. Miebaka, then nodded her head to her colleague, who stood up and began distributing copies of all the audits they had made from all incoming and outgoing transactions. These included the total profit and loss income statements made by the company, each month, for the last two and a half years.

Kate flashed a look at the account, who now had huge beads of sweat forming on his head. Her fingers trembled, as she held the A4 paper in her hand, trying every means possible to compose herself. She fanned herself with her hand, but her heart was racing very fast.

"Have we all gone through the report?" Mrs. Miebaka asked, looking sharply at all the staff members seated in the conference room.

"Yes, we have," they chorused.

"Alright. Well, ladies and gentlemen, I don't want to waste our time on this matter. What you are holding is a report containing the transactions that have occurred in this company for the last two and a half years.

"And from the analysis and calculations that have been made by my team, we've discovered that funds have been diverted from the company accounts to three different ones, which we have tracked. However, we quickly realized that these transactions had been tampered with, and deleted, so that they might not be traced."

At this point everyone was bewildered and surprised. They looked at each other and wondered who the guilty ones could be, while at the same time trying to avoid giving away any suspicious feelings.

Mrs. Miebaka continued, "Using our different tracking software, we have been able to retrieve these transactions, and the accounts these funds were forwarded into, in the past six months.

"As I mentioned earlier, there have been serious discoveries of underground looting. The following accounts have been traced and have received a whopping sum of ₦200,000 million in the last one year and four months: account numbers 0030912273, 0096543762, and 2413865797. The holders' names were stated as Jones Egba, Spiff Timi-pre, and Kate Udoh respectively."

As soon as the names were read out, the conference room came alive with murmurs from all angles. Kate stared into space in shock. Her feet trembled. She looked at the accountant, who had now bowed his bald head, in shame and disgrace.

You, bold vulture, she cursed him in her mind. She remembered the first day he had asked her to steal Mr. Dagogo's official stamp, so he could sign some checks in his name and send them to the bank. He had promised her she wouldn't get involved in all this.

The assurance was clear, and she had believed it. No one had ever mentioned any issue of missing funds from the company account since then, including the special bursary account given to the accountant to handle.

"Shit," Kate said loud enough for everyone to hear.

Kabiri Dan-Dagogo looked at her with bloodshot eyes. Each moment, as she tried to raise her head, she felt his dangerous eyes locking into hers and her skin. She felt that, if eyes could kill, she'd already be dead.

Kabiri fumed with anger and could be seen mouthing certain words to himself while Mrs. Miebaka was still talking. As a boss, he maintained his cool, just like the saying, "a lion doesn't make noise when it's hunting for its prey." He did not flinch one bit, but those who knew him could read the expression on his face as murder. They were afraid to meet his eyes, which were now red with anger.

Immediately the meeting ended, Kabiri Dan-Dagogo thanked the team of external editors and then called the guards at the gate, instructing them not to allow any TEMS Oil and Gas employees to leave the premises. He then walked angrily to his office without saying another word to anyone.

"You bastard, you told me I had nothing to worry about. See what troubles you've caused me." Kate said to the accountant Mr. Jones, pointing an accusing finger at him.

"Me? How was I supposed to know they had trackers and software in place that would detect the transactions?" he yelled back at her with clenched teeth and fist. "My whole life is ruined. What should I tell my wife and children?"

"Oh, so that's all you care about, huh? Have you thought of going to jail?" Kate panicked. Tears begin to run down her cheeks.

"You'd better fix this, Jones . . ."

"Fix what, Madam? We've been caught off guard and practically handicapped, can't you see? We are at the mercy of the boss. You heard him, right? No one leaves the premises," he said, breathing heavily.

Mr. Spiff sat quietly on a seat holding his peace.

Kate panted and paced the conference room to and fro. She bit her lower lip hard and snapped her fingers. "I won't go down alone; over my dead body; she got me into this mess, so she's going to go down with me."

The door flung open suddenly, and they all turned to face the door at the same time. "The boss wants you three in his office immediately." Timi informed them.

THIRTEEN

Kabiri Dan-Dagogo had not expected the accountant to be part of the fraudulent activities going on in the company. He had trusted Mr. Jones with huge amounts of money for years; never did he suspect a thing, until this drastic drop of sales and shortage of cash, a whopping sum of two hundred million naira stolen from him by staff members he'd thought were working for him.

Kate was even the last person he'd expected a betrayal from. And if anyone had told him that Kate would join his enemies to stab him in his back, he would have denied it with his life.

Although she was not as loyal as Mabel had been to him, Kate had worked with him longer than the rest. She had done her part by helping out so much to ensure that his job was smooth and easy. No woman is to be trusted after all, he thought as he kicked the visitor's chair in his office and pushed down the small pile of books.

A few minutes later, Kate, Mr. Jones, and Mr. Spiff walked into his office. He took his seat the moment they entered. All three had their eyes down in shame, and regret filled their countenance.

Drumming his fingers lightly on his desk, Kabiri Dan-Dagogo pushed those thoughts aside, so he could focus on what had happened and the people who had let this happen and were now standing before him. He shrugged and took a deep breath. None of the three culprits could utter a single word. They just stood and stared, unsure of his next line of action. He paused for a while, then asked them to sit.

The short knock on the door broke the long, awkward silence that filled the room. Timi walked majestically into the office with four brown envelopes in her hand and handed them over to Kabiri, who examined them carefully. He gave Timi a slight nod, and she turned to leave almost immediately.

"Are they here?" He asked, when she was halfway out of his office.

"Yes, Sir, about four of them."

Kabiri nodded coldly and waved a hand at her, then he passed the brown envelopes to each one of the culprits, their names carefully written on each one.

They turned to look at each other and back at the brown envelopes they held in their hands. Of course, they knew what the contents were.

"You all are fired." Kabiri said without any expression on his face.

"Eh!" Exclaimed Mr. Jones as he crossed his arms on his head as though he did not know the consequences of what he had done.

Kate blinked her eyes in utmost disbelief. She had been an accomplice only, but what she had received over the months was nothing compared to what her other partners in crime had been enjoying. This position at TEMS was the only source of livelihood she had, and if she was going down, then she mustn't go alone—Amina had to lose too. Kate would make sure she got the last laugh. She did not bother to open her letter. Just then, Timi led four policemen into the office. Kate's heart began to race; she panicked so much that her fingers began to tremble.

"Good day, Sir," one of the officers greeted Kabiri Dan-Dagogo.

"You're welcome," Kabiri responded as he rose from his sitting position.

"Well, these are the criminals," he said, pointing to the three of them (Kate, Jones, and Spiff). "You can do whatever you want with them. They are yours now." He said. "Make sure you use whatever it takes to retrieve as much money as you can from them."

The inspector turned to face the malefactors and he read out their rights to them, cuffed their hands behind them, and whisked them away to the waiting police van downstairs in company of the other three police escorts. Kate wept bitterly as she was being led out of the office; however, the moment they got to the door, she decided to let the cat out of the bag.

"I have a confession to make," she said loudly, tears streaming down her face as she spoke.

"What other damage could you have possibly done," Kabiri asked defensively.

"Please, Sir, if I don't say this, I would have to live with the guilt for the rest of my life."

She cried, "Em—I framed Mabel."

Kabiri's eyes brightened and his heart skipped at the mention of Mabel's name.

He let out a loud laugh, "Oh! Kate, you can't be serious right now?"

"I am telling the truth, Sir. The missing documents files for the Degema drilling site, that was all a setup masterminded by Amina."

Outraged that his fiancée's name was being brought into this matter, Kabiri shouted "Shut your mouth, you . . ." and he made to raise his hand to hit her, but was held back by the policeman who stood close to him.

"What?" He screamed.

Kate continued, "Amina has been giving me money to keep an eye on you. And any lady who comes close to you was reported to her. When Mabel came in, I got jealous because I wanted you too, and I hated the fact that she spends so much time with you on meetings, so I reported her to Amina, and we planned our little revenge on her.

"I stole the documents from her drawer and deleted all traces of the file from her computer." Kate said as she sulked and sobbed, choking occasionally at her own speech.

"Amina paid you to destroy my life?"

"No. . . . Sir, she paid me to frame Mabel up."

"At the detriment of my happiness and business?" he fumed; his jaw clenched.

"Get her out of my office, Officer. Please take her out before I do something crazy that I will regret later" he said. The police officers immediately did as he'd instructed and led Kate out of his office into their van.

Kabiri grabbed his car keys off his desk and stormed out of his office. He threw himself angrily on the driver's seat, then banged the door closed after him.

Revving up the streets in the car, he meandered into the express roadway and, in less than two hours, he was at Amina's apartment. He didn't honk his car horn, not sure if she was home, since he was too angry to speak with her over the phone.

He buried his face in his palms after he pulled over in front of Amina's apartment. He got out of his car, gently closing the door this time. He had to keep his cool and his temper under control.

The last time he had gotten so angry with a girl was during his junior school days. The girl had ended up at the school clinic and since then, he had vowed never to lay a finger on any woman, no matter the offense. He'd made a commitment to himself; History must not repeat itself. What baffled him the most was the fact that he had been in love with a devil all this while, without knowing it.

He banged aggressively on the apartment door.

"Who's that? Do you want to pull down the door?" He heard her scream from inside.

He continued banging on the door until she opened the door.

"Who the hell is that? Do you . . ." she paused her speech as she bumped into him.

"Baby! What's wrong?"

He grabbed her by the arm and took her inside before she could even complete her sentence.

"What are you doing, Kabiri? You're hurting me," she cried out.

He pushed Amina onto the couch. She bounced on it and began rubbing her hurting arm gently. Amina shot him a surprised gaze; confusion encapsulated her entire being.

"Amina, what did I do to you?" He asked almost in tears.

"What are you talking about?"

"Don't sit there and act like you don't know what you did, you heartless agent of the devil."

"Me?"

"Yes, you Amina, how dare you? With all the love and money I've given you, all you could come up with was to pay my staff to watch me? And, as if that wasn't enough, you got an innocent woman fired, to the detriment of my happiness and the good of the company."

"I'm sorry, Kabiri." She pleaded while attempting to hold his arm, but he snatched it away from her reach.

"You're sorry? Really, Amina? You played with my life and all I had worked for. Do you know the huge amount of money I have lost?"

Disgusted with himself and his own blindness, Kabiri said, "You know what, I don't even know why I am here talking to you. You deserve to rot in hell."

"Kabiri, don't do this to me! What about our wedding plans?"

"Wedding plans? You can have all of it. I don't care anymore," he said, walking out of the sitting room.

She ran along after him, pleading and begging. "I'm sorry. I'm so sorry," she cried. Her arms raised to her head.

"I'm sorry, I . . . I could talk to my father about . . ."

"You, your dad, and your entire family can go to hell, Amina. I don't care. And I don't want you to ever call me or come anywhere close to me again," he said and slammed his car door.

Amina jolted back in shock at the slam of the door. "What have I done?" she asked herself. She wanted to have Kabiri to herself; she did not expect things to escalate this far. "What will people say when they hear about this?" she asked herself again. She'd thought for a moment that she could win. Now, she realized that she had just dug her own grave with her own dainty hands and her long, perfectly pointed nails.

FOURTEEN

I t has been three months since the last audit. Kabiri had not recovered yet from his losses. First, it was Mabel. Then, the huge amount of money disappearing from the company account. Now, it was his relationship.

This certainly felt like starting from scratch, even though he still had his company. After employing new staff to fill in the emptied positions a month ago, he needed funds to run the company properly and effectively.

The Degema project had been placed on hold until he could get back on his feet. His father would not be happy with him because he had trusted Kabiri all his life when it came to managing the firm effectively. Now, due to this huge loss, some of the investors had withdrawn their funds. Kabiri understood that no one wanted to pump huge amounts of money into a company as incompetent as his. His brain went on and on to all kinds of ideas and strategies to bounce the company back to its former position at the top of the oil industry.

Kabiri could not get his mind settled on anything until the day Alex visited him at the office. Alex was the CEO of a tech company Kabiri Dan-Dagogo had been using for tech support at TEMS Oil and Gas for the past six years.

Each time Alex came to port Harcourt for some of his business meetings, he would always spend some quality time with

Kabiri before flying back to Abuja. He had heard of the drastic damage done by the former staff the day Kabiri called him.

Even though they had spoken over the phone, Kabiri Dan-Dagogo knew his friend for his adamant behavior. The day Alex visited, Kabiri had prepared a cup of hot chocolate for himself. He had just sipped a few times, before someone knocked on his office door.

Kabiri smiled the moment he heard the second knock, because that knock was unique to Alex. They had used it during their days at Lincoln University, in California.

Kabiri didn't bother to ask Alex to come in, because Alex would push the knob when he was done knocking.

"Guy, how have you been?" Alex asked, spreading his arms wide for a hug.

"Really?"

"Yes. C'mon, you need it more than I do" he said frantically.

Kabiri paused for a while letting Alex's arms hang on for a short while, before bracing them. They had a good time chatting about work and the situation. Kabiri explained all that had happened, but Amina's role in the entire game still baffled Alex.

"I can't seem to understand why some women are so delusional. Jeeeez!"

Kabiri only shook his head.

"Anyways, I heard from a reliable source that REN Petroleum Company is the real giant now in the oil and gas sector, and they are willing to sign partnerships with any other company if they are willing to share a 20 percent profit for a couple of years.

"And the good news is that the moment any company signed up with them, REN Petroleum would help the new company grow to become competent and strong enough to be able to stand on their own. What do you think?"

Kabiri shifted the pen he was holding from his left hand to his right, then he placed both hands on the table. This was definitely the best idea he had heard in the past eight weeks. He inhaled and exhaled heavily.

"Well, it's the best I've heard so far, and I do not have a choice. I think I will write to them later tonight and see if they would invite me for an interview or meeting or anything." He sighed.

"Okay. Here's their email address. A client of mine signed a four-year deal with them last week, so I thought you could give it a try too."

"Thanks, Bro, . . . I really appreciate it."

"You are welcome. Besides, it's what we do for brothers." They shook hands and, when Alex announced his departure, Kabiri walked him off to his car.

Back in his office, Kabiri pondered the idea and thought he'd give it a try.

He quickly tapped on his computer and drafted an application, attached some of the needed documents, and emailed the package to REN Petroleum at the email Alex had given him.

That done, Kabiri Dan-Dagogo took a deep breath and hoped all would turn out positive soon.

He sat there on his seat, with his thoughts running through several things he could have done if all was well with the company. Some of his abandoned projects were beginning to raise questions from the affected communities, as it was no longer news that he had gone bankrupt. The shocking thing was the resignation letters he'd got from two of his staff two weeks ago.

One had complained that the pay was no longer favorable to him anymore, as he had an entire family depending on him. After reading through the resignation letters, Kabiri laughed to himself.

Two nights later, while he scrolled through the list of emails he had received for the day, he had bumped into the email from REN Petroleum. Butterflies fluttered in his stomach, at the sight of that particular email. He could not wait for dawn to arrive.

They had sent a list of all the documents they would require to sign a contract with him.

If Kabiri and TEMS were found fit for a short-time merger agreement, they would gladly support him and help him get back on his feet. The terms and conditions were not stated in the email, but he was willing to give it a try. When it was dawn, he quickly prepared himself to drive down to the offices of the REN Petroleum Company.

The hugeness of the property and the buildings at the REN Petroleum campus made him pause for a moment. He thought he had all the money and the best opportunities for his staff to work with, but no, his firm was a mere joke compared to what he is seeing now. His meeting was scheduled for 10:00 a.m.

He pulled over at the exact spot directed by the security guard. When he got into the reception, he was given a visitor's tag on his suit and asked to use the elevator to the tenth floor. A young lady of about twenty-three years welcomed him and gave him a cup of coffee while he waited for his turn to meet the head of operations.

"You may go in, Sir," the young lady finally spoke to him again.

"Which way?" he asked gently.

"The third door by the right, Sir."

"Okay. Thank you."

Kabiri Dan-Dagogo walked majestically in the direction given to him. Along the way, he rearranged his suit and pressed his tie with his hands.

"Knock, knock." He tapped gently

"Come in, please," a sweet feminine voice spoke from inside. He turned the knob and walked in.

The lady had rolled her seat off to the other end of the desk in the huge office. She had a few files in her hands while she was bent over to focus on what she was looking for. She did not notice that the man had walked in.

"Good morning, Ma'am," he said in a calm voice.

"Good morning," she responded and turned her seat to face him.

"Mabel!" Kabiri's mouth went agape with shock and bewilderment, seeing her glammed up and looking all chic and gorgeous.

"Yes, Mr. Dan-Dagogo," she paused and watched him for a while before letting the words out of her mouth.

"You may have your seat, please."

CPSIA information can be obtained
at www.ICGtesting.com
Printed in the USA
BVHW051940220623
666272BV00005B/8/J